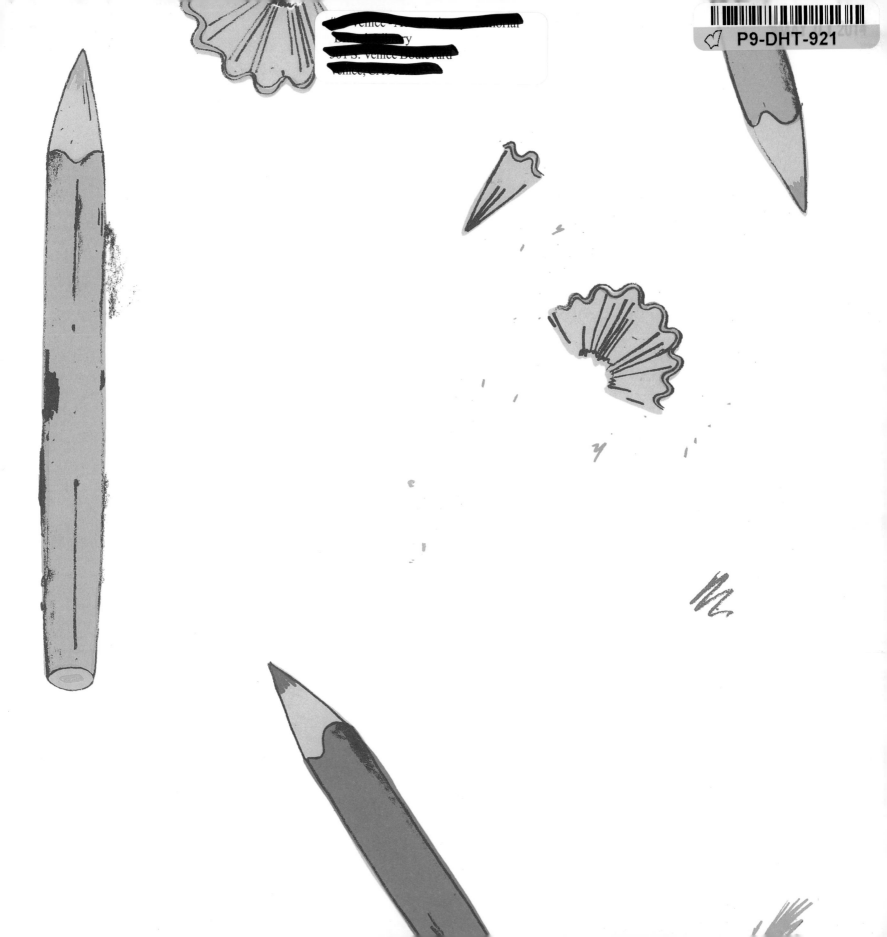

To Dicky and my lovely little Devin,
who will find his own way to say…
—N. R.

Special thanks to
Ailsa McWilliam

Ω

Published by
PEACHTREE PUBLISHERS
1700 Chattahoochee Avenue
Atlanta, Georgia 30318-2112
www.peachtree-online.com

First published in Great Britain in 2013 by Macmillan Children's Books, an imprint of Macmillan Publishers Ltd.
First United States version published in 2014 by Peachtree Publishers

The illustrations are screen prints

Printed in November 2013 in China
10 9 8 7 6 5 4 3 2 1
First Edition

Cataloging-in-Publication data is available from the Library of Congress

ISBN 978-1-56145-739-7 / 1-56145-739-6

natalie russell

Lost for Words

PEACHTREE
ATLANTA

Tapir had some pencils
and a nice new notebook.

But he didn't know
what to write.

He stared at the clean page and
tried to think of something. Anything!
But nothing popped into his head.
It felt empty, just like his page.

Tapir's friends could write words easily,
about things that meant a lot to them.

Giraffe was writing a poem
about his favorite tree. He chewed
its leaves as he wrote.

You are tall and thin, my perfect tree.

You reach so high, just like me!

Your leaves so juicy and good to chew,

Oh precious tree, I do love you.

Giraffe had
a way with words.

Hippo was in his muddy pool,
writing an exciting story.

Once upon a time there lived a very handsome hippo. One day, while dozing in the pool, he heard a bird cry for help. What a disaster! She was stuck in the mud! The very handsome hippo swam bravely to her rescue. "My hero," chirped Bird. Thank goodness the handsome hippo was an excellent swimmer.

THE END

Hippo always knew how to begin a story and how it would end. He was very clever.

Flamingo was composing
a song about the sun.
She hummed softly
as she wrote.

When the sun shines brightly in the sky,

I feel so happy, I want to fly!

I stretch my neck and fluff my feathers.

For me, sunshine is the best of weathers.

But when the clouds come and then the rain,

My long long legs become cold again!

Her song was so perfect it brought a tear to Tapir's eye.

I must be doing something wrong, thought Tapir.

So he tried humming

and wallowing.

He even chewed on
some juicy leaves.

But no words came.
The harder he tried,
the grumpier he felt.

"It's not fair!" said Tapir. "I don't know what to write!"

"Don't worry," said his friends. "You'll think of something."

But Tapir wasn't so sure.

He walked away…

...far away, to a quiet place on top of the hill.

Tapir looked out at the beautiful view
and began to think.

Then, very carefully, he opened his notebook and unpacked his pencils.

And without a word he drew the sun,
big and round, right at the top of his page—
a bright sun especially for Flamingo.

Under the sun Tapir drew the river,
long and winding, down to the pool
where Hippo liked to play.

He added plenty of mud
to keep Hippo happy.

Next to Hippo's pool, he drew
a tall tree. Tapir covered it in fresh
green leaves because he knew
Giraffe would like it that way.

When Tapir had finished, he looked proudly at what he'd drawn.

But there was something missing…

...three friends so important that
they needed a page all of their own!

Tapir rushed back to show his friends what he'd drawn.

"How wonderful you are!" said Giraffe.
"You draw so well," said Hippo.
"It's beautiful," whispered Flamingo,
wiping a tear from her eye.

Tapir didn't need words after all. Not one!

His colorful drawings said everything he wanted to say.

And they said it perfectly.